Good-bye, Hello!

by Shen Roddie

illustrated by Carol Thompson

DK Publishing, Inc.

Trenton Veterans Memorial Library
2790 Westfield Road
Trenton, MI 48183
734-676-9777

Good-bye, moon!

Hello, sun!

I wonder what I'll do today?

Good-bye, diaper!

Hello, potty!

Listen to the tinkling!

Good-bye,
highchair!

Hello, low chair!

I spy bananas for breakfast.

Good-bye, bottle!

Good-bye, baby food!

Hello, grown-up food!

Watch me eat my dinner.

Good-bye, booties!

Hello, shoes!

I'm ready for a walk.

Good-bye, stroller!

Hello, feet!

What a lot
to see!

Good-bye, Mom!

Hello, friends!

We're off to the moon!
Boom! Boom!

Good-bye, crib!

Hello, bed!

One jump and I'm up!

There are no good-byes
when it's time for my nap,
because it's always